Corny: A F/F Candy Corn Romance

By Sabrina Cross

To everyone who looked at an inanimate object and said 'yeah, I could fuck that.'
You inspire and terrify me every day.

Chapter One

"No one said anything about a sacrifice," Fern yelped.

"Oh, calm down. It's not like we're going to be sacrificing a goat. It's just a prick to your finger, a drop of blood, and you're done. Although, if you could take a prick we wouldn't have to be doing this." Violet's response was typically blunt and abrasive.

"Leave Fern alone," Jasmine said, pulling her long, dark hair into a messy knot on the top of her head. "There's nothing wrong with her."

"She's a twenty-six-year-old virgin. There's a lot wrong with her." Violet huffed. She caught my glare and turned her attention back to the old, faded book in her lap.

I guess I should start at the beginning.

First, let me assure you that we are most definitely not getting ready to sacrifice a goat. Or a cat, or even a frog. For one thing, I wouldn't even know where to find a goat. And for another, I wouldn't want to have to clean up the blood. Oh, and have you seen goats? They're freaking adorable. Who would want to sacrifice one of the cutest animals on the planet? Straight up, evil people, that's who.

My friends and I aren't evil. Well, Violet might be able to claim the title of Villainess, but she's yet to actually murder anyone or anything. She can't even bring herself to kill spiders. She catches them and takes them outside. We're not even witches, despite what things look like.

You see, a few weeks ago, the four of us went on a drive. We didn't have any particular location in mind, but wanted to get out of town for a bit. We stopped anywhere that looked interesting. We hit up yard sales, thrift stores, antique malls, craft fairs. We'd spent the whole day just driving around and wandering places. That was when Violet found the book.

At one of the yard sales we stopped at was a gorgeous old oak chest Fern wanted, but it was filled with all kinds of crap. And the lady holding the yard sale said if we took the chest, we had to take everything in it too. She was selling her grandmother's things to help pay for the nursing home she was now living in, which cost an arm, a leg, and a first born child to get her into.

Fern agreed, and we loaded the chest into the back of Jasmine's mini van and off we went. No one thought about it again for a few days until Fern started going through the chest.

There were old books, a bunch of crystals, some oddities like small bones and feathers and stuff. There was a bunch of musty fabric, some half-burned candles, and some very old and gross yarn, along with a set of crochet hooks. Well, Violet, the book nerd of the group, claimed the books right away. The crochet hooks came to me, the only one of the group who knew how to use them.

They were actually really nice hooks. Made of some kind of wood, they'd been smoothed and polished and were smoother than any wooden hooks I've used in the past. I typically preferred metal, but these were a really nice set.

Well, it turns out that the lady's grandma must have been a witch, because the books were all handwritten journals with spells and incantations and uses for different herbs and crystals. It was kind of interesting, though I didn't have much belief in the reality of magic. I'd enjoyed flipping through them with Violet.

Anyway, that's how this all began. While the rest of us had written the books and contents of the chest off, Violet had apparently been studying the books closely. She had found a spell to "break our dry streaks" as she put it.

Now, personally, I was fine with my single-ness and prolonged celibacy. And Jasmine's divorce hadn't been finalized all that long ago in the grand scheme of things. Plus, Fern wasn't exactly waiting for marriage, but she was also really, really picky when it came to men. But Violet had been in the dating pool for months now, and honestly, dating as a millennial just sucked.

Which was why I was fine being single. Who needed the drama?

But it was coming up on Violet's thirtieth birthday and she was stressing the big three-oh and being single and wanting kids so we'd all agreed to humor her. Although we may have done so less readily if we'd known self-stabbing was involved…

It was the last full moon before Violet's birthday in three weeks and she insisted we do it now. She'd tried to insist we do it at midnight, since everyone apparently knows that spells work best at midnight. Frankly I wasn't staying up that late and Jasmine's babysitter would quit on the spot.

Which is why four women who couldn't look less like witches found themselves sitting in a circle on my living room floor on a Thursday evening.

There was Jasmine, the mom of the group, in her black skinny jeans and light pink polo shirt, playing up her warm brown skin. Her dark brown waves pulled up into a knot on the top of her head. Violet, the short and brash one (wasn't it always the short ones?) with her jeans and t-shirt demanding the reader "read banned books." She was curvy, currently rocking purple hair, and had the prettiest hazel eyes I'd ever seen.

Fern was the youngest of us by a few years and the perfect girl next door. She was in a light blue sundress with her long, curly blond hair braided to one side to hang over her shoulder. She had a smattering of freckles and bright blue eyes.

Finally, there was me, the giant. At just shy of six feet with curves for days, I wasn't one you could miss in a crowd. I was the only one of us who would pass as a witch with my dyed black hair, vivid red lips, short black dress, and Victorian style boots. Yeah, I was a goth. But I figured if people wanted to stare, I'd give them something to stare at. Plus, I looked hot AF.

"Okay everyone, when I say to, light the candle in front of you. I'm going to say the spell, you guys repeat it back to me. We're going to take our papers and burn them to send our intentions out into the universe. Stay focused on what you want in your future partner. Once they're burned, we'll dump the ashes into the bowl and each put in three drops of blood. There's some herbs and stuff that I have to add, we blow out the candles and then we bury the ashes in the yard. Easy."

"Oh, yes, easy." Jasmine intoned. While she didn't physically roll her eyes, it was implied.

"You don't really expect me to stab myself with that knife, do you?" Fern asked.

"Yes, I do. It'll be fine! Look, I even have bandaids all ready." Violet held up the small tin of bandages with a unicorn on it. Aweeeeesome. "Okay, everyone ready?"

I picked up my lighter. "Ready."

***

"Well, that was a bust." Violet whined as she finished packing up the supplies she'd brought for the spell.

"What, did you expect a hoard of men to break down Clover's door?" Jasmine asked. She was sitting in my oversized reading chair, her legs pulled up under her.

"No, but maybe some candle flickering or something to know the spell worked."

"I'm actually really OK that it didn't," Fern said from her place next to me on the couch. "Who needs men anyway?"

"If you would let me help you get laid, you'd understand why we need men."

"Ahem," I stabbed the crochet hook through the loop of yarn. "Not all of us need men."

"Okay, but Fern isn't bi or into women. She's just incredibly stubborn."

"It's called having standards, Violet." Jasmine said, "Maybe if you tried having some, you wouldn't be trying to use the dark arts to get yourself a boyfriend."

Jasmine had a point. Violet was historically unpicky when it came to men, and she seemed to always make the worst choices possible. It's why Fern and Jasmine both had access to her dating profiles. They vetted all of her dates before she was allowed to meet them.

Since my history with men was equally abysmal, I kept myself out of Violet's dating life.

"Clover, what the fuck is that?" Jasmine asked suddenly. I grinned and flipped my current WIP (that's work-in-progress) around for everyone to see.

It was hands down the most ridiculous thing I had ever made, and I loved it so hard. I only had a few more rows to go before I was done, and I couldn't wait to get pictures up for my fellow fiber artists to appreciate.

"That's…" Fern trailed off, her hand flying to her mouth to bite off a laugh.

"Clover, just why?" That was from Jasmine. She was staring in horror at my creation, but she couldn't help the smile trying to fight its way out.

"Okay, you've got to make me a hooker candy corn when you're done with that one. I need it to go with my penis and tits collection." Both of which I had crocheted for Violet.

I held the candy corn away from me and appreciated my handiwork. The thing was about two feet tall with black hooker boots, an ass that any woman would envy, and tits for days. I'd emphasized its features with a black thong and triangle bikini top. It was still three months to Halloween but I knew this one was going to be a hit on my website.

That's what I did. I sold crochet patterns and made crochet stuffies, specifically grown-up themed items. I was most well known for my "pocket rocket" (aka a penis but lord knows you can't use that word on social media) and boob pillows. I had a bunch of normal patterns, but it was the adult stuff that paid my bills.

"You are absolutely certifiable. The both of you." Jasmine said. "On that note, I'm heading home. If I leave now, I can shave an hour off of what I have to pay the babysitter. Fern, do you want a ride home?"

"That'd be great." Fern lived in an apartment complex not far from my house, so she often just walked over, but it was on the way for Jasmine.

"Yeah, I'm going to take off too. I have some papers I need to grade tonight."

Yeah, that's right. Violet is one of the people shaping young minds as a teacher. I fear for our society.

After they were gone, I poured myself a glass of red wine and turned on one of my favorite horror movies. I worked on finishing my candy corn as I watched the masked murderer stalk and torment his victims on screen.

Chapter Two

I jerked awake and then swore loudly as I fell off the couch onto the wood floor, getting wedged between the couch and the coffee table. I must have fallen asleep at some point last night after I wove in the loose ends of my crochet project, but before the movie ended.

Ugh, my hip was already starting to hurt. I got my arm under me and started pushing to my feet, wondering what it was that had woken me up. I looked around the dark room but didn't see anything out of place.

Using the couch and the table, I shoved to my feet. I pulled up the left side of my skirt to see the skin already turning red. Damn it. I dropped my skirt.

"You should pull that back up. I was enjoying the view." A low, smokey female voice said.

I screamed and spun in a circle, trying to locate the source of the voice. Someone was in my house. They were in my house and they were objectifying me. What the actual hell?

"Down here." I spun back around, looking down toward the couch where the voice came from. The only thing there was the candy corn stuffy I had finished earlier that night. "Yeah, that's right."

The voice…

The voice was coming from the candy corn. My stuffed candy corn hooker was talking to me.

I was clearly dreaming. Or hallucinating. Yeah, I was hallucinating.

"You're not hallucinating." The candy corn shoved away from the back of the couch to stand on its two legs. Something it physically should not have been able to do. "Or dreaming."

"What…how…huh?"

"You humans, always so eloquent. You summon a demon, a demon shows up, and you act like you've no clue what's going on." The candy corn scrunched its face in a glare.

It didn't have a face. I didn't give the candy corn face, but I knew in the very fiber of my being that that stuffy was glaring at me.

"What do you mean demon? I didn't summon anything!"

My mind flashed to all of us sitting in a circle, trying to summon our perfect partners.

"Ah, I see you're getting it now." The candy corn leaned forward, shoving the tip of its head under the edge of my skirt. I slapped my skirt down and stepped back, forgetting that the coffee table was behind me. I ended up landing on my butt on the table.

"Awww, you're no fun. I just wanted another peek." The candy corn straightened up. "Yep, you and your nitwit friends, you see what I did there? Summoned me, and now I'm here to help fulfill the terms of your bargain."

"There was no bargain!" I'd remember something like that. All we'd done was put our wish out in the world, not sign a contract.

"You signed in blood, you idiot human." The candy corn stuffy was swaying forward and back on its little legs. Something about its behavior screamed delight and all of the hair on my body stood on end.

What the hell has Violet done to us?

"If you're going to just sit there, why don't you open your legs. I only got a peek before, but I'd love to see more." There it goes again, objectifying me.

"I'm good, thanks." I ground out between clenched teeth. "What, exactly, are the terms of this bargain we made?"

The candy corn scoffed. And somehow scowled. How was it making facial expressions without a face?

"You all asked for true love. You each have one year to find true love, or your lives are forfeit, and your souls belong to Lucifer. And to make things extra fun, each of you will be assigned a demon to 'help' things along. Think of me as your personal fairy godmother."

This could not actually be happening. I could not be having a conversation with a talking caked out stuffed candy corn. I did not sign my soul away so Violet could get laid.

Oh gods, did I sign my soul away just so Violet could get laid?

Chapter Three

"Why haven't the others gotten their demon?" It'd been 48 hours since I'd woken up to find a talking candy corn on my couch and I'd learned quite a bit in that time.

One: No matter how much I wanted to believe I was just going crazy, there actually was a demon possessing my caked out candy corn.

Two: The demon's name was Callaxis but preferred that I called her Candy.

Three: She was a succubus and had been delighted to learn she would be getting to spend all of her time 'helping' me find true love.

Four: She drank coffee like a trucker.

No, I had no clue how the being with no arms or mouth managed to drink coffee. I'd woken up the last two mornings to a fresh pot that was thick as tar and tasted about as good as drinking old tires.

I'd looked up succubus after she'd dropped that information and learned it was a female demon that fed on lust. Which explained why she was always trying to look up my skirt or watch me in the shower, I guess. Apparently, the male counterpart was an incubus. Since I was bisexual, they'd assigned me a succubus.

Lucky, lucky me.

Not that I thought having a male demon would be any better than Candy. It was just that the female demon was grating on my every last nerve. Violet had been spending all of her time trying to figure out what went wrong and how to get out of the bargain. So far, she hadn't had any luck. Nor had any of them had demons pop up in their lives.

"Because you haven't made them vessels yet. You should really get on that, you know. The clock is ticking for your friends too." Candy was sitting on the couch while I was curled up in my chair across from her.

I kept the table between us. I did my best to keep something between us at all times or else she was trying to get under my skirts or into the leg holes of my shorts. Goddamn demon was a perv with zero sense of personal boundaries. She'd even snuck into my bed last night and I had zero clue how she'd managed it since I had locked the door, and my bed was on the tall side.

But I'd woken up with her snuggled against my front, my arm thrown over her like a teddy bear. I had another bruise on my hip from getting tangled in the blankets as I flung myself out of bed.

"What do you mean I haven't made them yet?"

"You have the wand." She nodded toward my hands, where I was using one of the crochet hooks to make a giant hot pink penis roughly the size of a small child. It was a custom order, and who was I to judge? I was talking to a caked-out candy corn.

"Are you telling me you only exist because I made you using the crochet hooks I found in that trunk?" I looked down at the hook in my hand. It was pretty and all, but nothing particularly fancy.

"They're made from a sacred tree. They're used to make poppets. Or, in this case, to give hell a humanesque form."

"You're really stretching the definition of humanesque here." I had a feeling if Candy had a tongue, she'd be sticking it out at me.

"Anyway, you have to give them form. I suggest you don't turn them into giant phalluses. We may be stuck in wool bodies, but we maintain many of our powers and I'd hate to see anything happen to you before you are given a chance to find your mate."

"Why would you want me to find my mate? Isn't the point of you to ensure my soul for the devil?" I swapped the hook I was using on the pink penis to an old metal one. I wasn't positive I believed her, but also, I wasn't going to risk being incinerated because I accidentally summoned a demon into a giant penis.

"Technically, but I'm also a demon of lust. If you find your mate, then I get to feed on all of that delicious lust. I get to be well-fed through you or I get to steal your soul. Either way, I win." I shuddered at the idea of Candy sitting on my dresser, feeding on me having sex with someone.

"Won't Lucifer be mad if you don't bring me back?" My hands worked the yarn quickly, trying to ignore the twisting in my stomach every time I thought about the pact with the devil we had unknowingly made.

"Eh, what's one puny human soul? He'd hardly notice, honestly."

I supposed there was some comfort in that.

If I could believe her.

As I worked on the stuffy, I thought about what I could make to give my friends their demons. Or even if I should. Would we be punished if we never gave the demon form? Would they feel the same way as Candy and be happy if we did manage to find love? Where the hell did one find love in the twenties? The very idea of a dating app made me want to just give up and yeet myself to Lucifer's feet.

"Yeah, I would avoid dating apps if I were you. They're good ole Luci's brain child and designed to torture humans. You'll have to figure out how to find love the old-fashioned way."

"Oh, joy!"

Chapter Four

"Did you find anything in the journals, Violet?" Jasmine asked. "Anything to confirm or deny what Candy told Clover?"

We were at a local bar on a Friday night. Something none of us would have willingly done, but we were on a timeline to find love and this seemed as good a place as any. Well, in theory. In reality, we were anti-social creatures that didn't know how to interact with the general public, or people over the age of ten.

"As far as I can tell, no one ever cast that spell before. Unless there are missing journals, there is nothing to indicate Harriet ever went through with it. I'm not sure if it's because she met Gary before she did it. Or if she met Gary because of the spell and just never wrote about it. She stopped practicing about the time she got married so it would explain the lack of entries. She packed everything into her trunk and there it stayed until Fern just *had* to have it."

"Don't lay this on me!" Fern said. "I'm not the one who decided casting spells to get laid was a fun way to spend a Thursday night. I hadn't even wanted to do the spell and now look at us!"

The bar was one of those places that couldn't decide if it was a family restaurant or a proper bar and fell into this awkward in-between area. We were sharing a blooming onion and jalapeno poppers, and had a pitcher of questionable margaritas for the table.

"That's not the point," Jasmine said. "The point is, we don't know if Clover's demon is telling the truth."

"She's not my demon!" I ground out, but no one was listening to me. They had all handled Candy's existence with the same grace I had. Jasmine just sat there stuttering "what" over and over again. Fern had fainted, and Violet had immediately started poking the crochet candy corn looking for a sound box or speaker, certain I was faking it somehow. In the end, like me, they'd had no choice but to believe that she was what she claimed to be, and the bargain was real. None of us knew what to do about it.

"I've decided I'm going to trust her." I said, taking a long drink of my margarita. "I am going to believe that the bargain is real, and the timeline is real and that somehow each of us will meet our true love over the course of the next year. The trick will be identifying them."

"I think it's safe to assume that the demons aren't actually here to help us." Jasmine said.

"Probably not. They're probably here to act as a stumbling block, a distraction, a way to lead us away from them so that Lucifer can claim us," Violet said, then laughed. "This is a real conversation I'm having."

"Yes, get over it." Jasmine snapped. "You got us into this mess and we're going to have to figure a way out of it."

"First thing we need to do is each of you need to decide on a form for your demons. Candy said the crochet hooks are meant to make poppets and whatever I make with them will act as a vessel. She also warned me her demon brethren don't have as much of a sense of humor as her and you should probably avoid picking something like a candy cake hooker or a giant penis."

"Can I have a life-sized werewolf?" Violet asked. At my side-eye, she shrugged. "What? If I'm going to be stuck with some sort of sex demon, I want it to be interesting at least."

"I guess. It'll take a while though. Anyone else have any requests?"

"If she gets a werewolf can I have a giant teddy bear?" Jasmine asked. "I've always wanted one."

"Why not? Fern?"

"Can I get back to you?" She looked thoughtful in a way that the others hadn't been. As if the form her demon took really mattered to her.

I shrugged.   "I guess. But don't take too long in deciding. It's already been a week, and the clock is ticking for all of us."

Chapter Five

We went out to local bars and events almost every night, trying to find someone, anyone, interesting enough to even consider dating, let alone be my true love. What even was true love? That was some fairy tale bullshit that no one could define. So how were we even supposed to know what we're looking for?

"You're so tightly wound." Candy said one night after I got home from the bar with my friends. It had been a total bust and Violet had ended up elbowing a guy in the gut after he refused to accept Fern's timid no as an answer. No true love there.

"Yeah, well, I've got quite a bit going on now, don't I?" I unlaced my boots and sighed when I finally pried them from my feet. They were pointed and heeled ankle boots, cute as fuck but so not comfortable for long-term wear.

I tugged a strap of the black pinafore down over my shoulder, and then the other, before turning to see Candy resting on the end of my bed. It was one of her preferred places to rest, along with the right side of my couch and in my oversized chair.

Over the last couple of weeks we'd fallen into something of a routine and I was more than a little disturbed at times how easily I rolled with having a candy corn hooker possessed by a demon as a roommate.

"Don't stop on my account," Candy said, nodding to where my hand still gripped the second strap of my dress. "You know, I rather enjoy being snuggled up to you most nights, but I'll admit I'd love to see the whole package."

Yes, I'd given up trying to keep the demon out of my bed. The last time I shoved her to the floor after waking up with her tucked in next to me, she shoved back. Except she'd waited until I'd fallen back asleep to do it and I'd been startled awake by the impact of my ass hitting the ground and my head banging into the end table.

"Pass." I dropped the strap and moved to my dresser to find pjs. I'd change in the bathroom.

"You know, I've been here for almost three weeks, and you haven't orgasmed once in that time. It's no wonder you're wound so tight. Don't you know that an orgasm a day keeps the doctor at bay?"

"That's an apple, you horny bitch." I ground out. I was well aware of how long it had been since my last orgasm. But there was no way I was going to jill off with Candy in audience and the demon never left me alone long enough to get anywhere. I'd tried in the shower last week, but I am not someone who can come quickly and she'd been yelling through the door before I even got close.

"What the hell is an apple going to do? Orgasms improve heart health, raise white blood cell count, and boost endorphins, making you happy. And girl, you could use some happy."

I was getting a positive benefits of sex lecture from a goddamn crochet candy corn with a better ass than me. Why was this my life?

"You'd be doing us both a favor, you know." Candy said as I started to cross to my en suite bathroom.

"Yeah? And how's that?" If voices could drip, skepticism would be pouring off of mine.

Candy shifted on the bed, and then again. There was an air of uncertainty about her, and the demon was never uncertain. Bossy, arrogant, horny, demeaning, but never uncertain.

"Okay, look, I haven't been topside in a long, long time. Which means I haven't fed in forever. Normally I'd just go seduce an idiot man to get what I need, but obviously that wouldn't work while I'm bound to this ridiculous form." She 'looked,' down at her body. Though I was certain she couldn't see below the giant tits, I'd given her. She was wearing the white dress I'd made her. It went almost to the floor and made her overly large chest and ass look comically huge.

"What does that have to do with me masturbating?"

"It's not as good as banging it out, but I can feed off of the sexual energy in the room. It's a win-win. You get to orgasm and calm the fuck down, and I finally get a little sustenance." Her voice, normally low and smokey and honey smooth, carried a thread of anger in it. As if asking me for what she needed was beneath her.

A large part of me wanted to say fuck you and let the demon starve. But there was a part of me that felt for her. And there was a denied part of me that really, really wanted that orgasm.

I turned back and dropped my clothing on the bedside table. I had a feeling I was going to regret this. But I couldn't not help her. It wasn't like she was here by choice any more than I was. She'd told me Lucifer himself had assigned her to watch over me. Something highly terrifying to me, but rather significant for her, I'd gathered.

"You can't watch me. That's too creepy." I said, sliding up onto the bed. Candy made an awkward turn and leaned her 'head' against the footboard.

"Are you going to touch yourself for me, little human?"

"Don't sound so smug." I shifted to where my back was against the pillows. Reaching for the phone I'd tossed on the bed earlier I pulled up my favorite Tumblr blog. I wasn't a huge fan of video porn, but the things people on Tumblr could do with a gif and a well-worded caption was enough to get me there almost every time.

I shifted on the bed, spreading my legs slightly as I used my hand to slowly slide my black pinafore skirt up my thighs. I read a short story based on a black and white gif while I toyed with the edge of my underwear before sliding my hand up to brush across my breasts.

"You have the sexual energy of a nun." Candy said, shifting as though to turn around.

"Turn around and that's all you'll get. Have you never heard of edging into it?" I tugged my shirt up to pluck at my nipple through the thin white lace.

"I've heard of edging. I'm more of a flash fire sort of girl, myself."

"Well, I'm not. So shut up or go away so I can get ready for bed." I would cry if I had to stop. My nipples were already pebbled into hard points and becoming more sensitive by the moment. I pinched one, just hard enough for the edge of pain but not enough to make me cry out. I may be sharing my sex energy with Candy, but I wasn't comfortable enough to be loud with her.

"I'll shut up. Please don't stop." Her voice was needier than I felt. I needed to fix that.

I slid my hand down over the rounded curve of my stomach and under my skirt. I debated taking my white lace panties off, but decided against it, sliding my hand under them instead. It added to the illicit feeling I was having, which was more arousing than I thought it would be.

I'd never been the most adventurous in bed. I had a minor praise/degradation kink, and I liked a little edge of the good kind of pain, but I had never liked the idea of being on display or watched or anything. Yet something about Candy being in the room was egging me on. I kept silent, but a part of me wanted her to hear me. I was a mess of conflicting emotions that I needed to shove aside if I wanted this orgasm.

My vulva was soft and warm and smooth under my hand. I slid my fingers along my slit and down. I teased my opening, dampening my fingers, before sliding my hand back up to find my clit. I gently circled around it, not quite touching but giving the impression of pressure.

I scrolled my phone until I found another of my favorite writers. As I read their short story, I pressed one finger softly to the aching bundle of nerves circling it slowly toward the center before taking it between two fingers and gently squeezing. My hips arched off the bed as I found just the right spot and pressure.

One of my favorite things about masturbating over having sex is when I find the right spot, I stay there. Unlike when you're with someone else, and you say "right there, don't stop" and, for some godforsaken reason, they always, always change what they're doing. And the orgasm that was so close, was now out of reach.

When I find the spot, I don't move until the pressure is too much and the hollow, aching feeling in my cunt overrides everything but the need to be filled and I drive my fingers into myself.

The soft sound of my fingers driving in and out of my wet hole was obscene. My breathing was jagged, and it was taking so much effort to stay silent. I dropped my hand holding my phone, no longer needing assistance to get into the mood. Instead, I looked down at Candy at the end of the bed, her little wool candy corn body nearly vibrating in time with my body.

A dangerous part of me wants to beg her to turn around, wants her to see what I'm doing to myself. I slam it down just as my fingers find and press on that place just inside my opening that always makes my eyes roll back and my brain go numb. This time I can't bite back the sound as I come on a moan. I vaguely hear Candy moaning along with me.

After pushing myself through the orgasm, I look back down, but the candy corn demon is gone. And for some reason, I cannot explain, I feel very alone.

Chapter Six

Another week passes and neither Candy or I speak about what took place in my bedroom that night. We both act like it never happened. During that time, I finished the giant blue and purple octopus Fern requested and delivered it to her. Candy assured me Fern's incubus would take possession of the cursed stuffy when it was time to do so. I thought the time had already long passed as I'd had my demon pest for weeks now, but apparently no one else agreed.

Meanwhile, Violet kept searching for a way out of the bargain, though I'd begun losing hope we ever would. Instead, I focused my attention on finding dates. I'd had a meet-cute at the coffee shop over a mixed up coffee order (the barista had mixed up my drink with Calvin's) and had a date planned for that night.

"I haven't had a date with a man in five years." I told Candy as I stood in my closet doorway wearing nothing but my towel. "What does one even wear on a date anymore?"

We'd jokingly decided not to get coffee, and were meeting at a local pub with the idea we could get drinks. And if it didn't suck, we could grab some dinner while we were there. It was practical and logical and a part of me absolutely hated all of the idea.

But I didn't have the luxury of time and maybe Calvin was just being so pragmatic since it was a first date, and first dates are always scary and stressful.

Maybe he wasn't always so boy scout prepared and logical about everything. Or maybe those traits would balance my admittedly freewheeling ways.

"As little as possible." Candy suggested from her spot on the bed, her black skirt bunched around her.

I still hadn't quite figured out how she managed to get onto the bed herself. Or the couch. Or drink the pots of coffee she went through every day. I'd watched her, and it was like she was standing on the floor one minute and on the bed the next without appearing to move. I realize she is a demon and that shouldn't shock me, but it always did.

"I'm not sure I want to take fashion advice from a candy corn hooker." I said over my shoulder. I pulled out a black sundress with cap sleeves and a corset back and held it up to my chest, debating.

"You're the one who put me in this body. My real form is glorious," Candy huffed. "And any idiot knows if you want to seduce a man, you just show some skin. Not that one. It's too long."

It fell just below my knees. I wondered what a succubus thought was an appropriate length. Just long enough to cover my butt?

"Wear the red one." Candy said. I turned to look at her. She was leaning over on the bed, clearly trying to see around me into the closet.

I put the black dress back and pulled out the red one. It had thin straps, a button front bodice and a swing skirt that fell about three inches short of my knees. It was bright, stop-light red and had been a clearance purchase in a moment of sheer insanity. The tags still dangled from the armpit.

"It's not really my color." I said, putting it back. The dress flew off the hanger and into my face.

"It is exactly your color. Wear the damn dress." I spun to glare at Candy, who was letting off an air of amused innocence I wasn't buying for a moment. "What? Did you think I only had the ability to get on furniture and cook breakfast? You have no clue what I'm capable of. So put the damn dress on, do your makeup and go see if this pathetic human is your soulmate."

I grumbled under my breath about know-it-all demons and finding a priest to do an exorcism as I stomped to the bathroom. When I came out twenty minutes later in the red dress and my makeup on, there was a pair of flats, a silver anatomical heart pendant, and a small coffin-shaped crossbody purse sitting on my bed. Oh goodie, the demon was accessorizing me now too.

Candy was nowhere to be seen as I finished getting dressed (yes, in the accessories she'd laid out because they were cute) and moving my essentials to the coffin purse. I'd expected her to be sitting on the couch or in the kitchen with her coffee, to crow about how fantastic I looked. Because I did look fantastic, damn it.

But I didn't see her anywhere before I had to leave for my date.

After weeks of her constantly being in my space, offering her endless unwanted opinions, it felt a little weird not to see her before I left. I tried to shake the feeling off in the uber on the way to the pub, but that sense of something being off lingered.

Oh great, I was becoming attached to the demon-possessed crochet hooker candy corn.

Just when I thought life couldn't get weirder.

***

I stumbled through the doorway, the sudden loss of the door to support me, leaving me unbalanced. I laughed as Calvin caught me around the waist before sliding his hands up to cup my breasts. He pressed a kiss to my shoulder, and I sighed, leaning back into him.

"So, this is my house. It's nothing special, but it's mine." And it was. I'd inherited the two-bedroom house from my grandmother when she passed away a few years back. It had taken me years to change it from her house to my home, and pieces of her still remained. Like the sprawling landscape painting in the entryway that had been there most of my life, currently askew.

Calvin rolled my right nipple in his fingers, and I stopped thinking about Grandma and the painting and basically any thoughts at all. He nudged me forward with his body far enough to get the door closed. The next thing I knew, our positions had flipped, and I was pressed up against the wall with Calvin pressed against me and his tongue down my throat.

The room was spinning and tilting from the sudden movement, and Calvin wasn't a particularly good kisser. I was debating my level of horny versus my lack of actual interest in having sex with this man, when suddenly he was no longer pressed against me. Calvin was crumpled on the floor in a heap, like his bones had just given out, and he went down. Except he hadn't made a sound, and he had seemed fine just moments ago.

Was he more drunk than I thought? It's possible. I was pretty drunk myself. We'd foregone dinner in favor of drinking and chatting. By the time he worked his way up to kissing me, I'd already determined it probably wasn't true love and he was just as boring and pragmatic as he originally seemed. It just so happened I was also too drunk to care that there was little chance of a future here. It has been five years since I'd been with a guy, two-point-five since I broke up with my last girlfriend, and I just wanted someone to touch me.

Except now, he was laying on the floor and the room was spinning, and I thought I might throw up. Oh gods, was he dead?

"He's not dead." Candy was standing in the doorway to the living room. "He's going to wish he was dead when he wakes up, though."

"Damn it, Candy! I thought I told you to stay out of my head!" She'd changed into a red dress (again, don't ask me how the armless stuffy managed it. Just roll with it.) and if she had a face she'd be glaring at me right now. I glared back.

"I wasn't. Your face just said it all."

"What did you do to him?" I demanded, stepping over Calvin's body to stalk toward the demon.

"Nothing he didn't deserve." Candy turned her glare to the man slumped on my entryway floor. "That man was planning on using you and never calling again. He's got a wife and two kids and a damned dog. And even if he wasn't the worst sort of asshole, who the hell gets a woman drunk and takes advantage of her? Creeps, that's who!"

I froze, propping one hand on the doorway to keep myself upright. Okay, so maybe she had saved me from making a terrible mistake. Still, it was my mistake to make.

"What if I wanted to be taken advantage of?" I demanded. Candy's attention swung back to me. I couldn't read her like I usually could. "What if, for once, I just wanted someone else to be the one touching me? What if I'm tired of being the only one to get me off? What if I give zero fucks that he's married and just wanted to get laid?"

"Oh, little human, you deserve so much more than whatever this limp-wrist asshole could give you." Her voice was low, thick, and tugged at something low in my stomach. "Now please open the door and I'll take out the trash. Also, you'll want to get your keys out of the lock."

It took some effort with Calvin in the way but I got the door open and my keys from the lock without losing the contents of my stomach. As soon as I stepped back to put my keys in the bowl on the side table, Calvin was in movement.

He didn't get up and walk out, though. No, it was like someone had grabbed both feet and was dragging him out of the house. As soon as he was clear of the door, it slammed shut and the deadbolt turned.

Candy was much scarier than I gave her credit for.

Suddenly uncomfortable with the demon in a way I hadn't been before, I edged toward the hallway and my bedroom. Not that locks had been effective in keeping her out before, but I needed a moment of privacy to think. I also possibly needed to throw up.

Chapter Seven

Candy was on my bed when I stumbled out of the bathroom a while later. I'd spent some time lying on the floor with my overheated face pressed against the cold tile until the panic and nausea receded. I'd used a washcloth to wipe my makeup off and tugged my hair up into a knot on top of my head, but couldn't be bothered to do anything else.

"You're scared of me now." Candy said. She was resting back against my pillows, her black dress from earlier exchanged for a red one that matched mine. If she wasn't possessed, you'd think she was any stuffed animal that belonged there.

A part of me had gotten used to her being there. I'd grown too comfortable with the demon and had forgotten what she was.

"You know what I am." Candy said simply. "My job is to keep you safe long enough for Lucifer to claim your soul. I take my job very seriously."

"You're saying he was going to harm me?"

"There are a lot of ways to harm someone. He was a threat to your mental well-being." I shuffled to the bed, still in my dress, and tried to pick Candy up to move her away from my pillows. But she suddenly felt like she was made of solid lead. She was still soft and squishy but so dense and heavy I couldn't budge her.

Whatever. I shoved the blankets down and crawled onto the bed, turning my back to the demon, I tugged the blanket up over my head to discourage any more conversation.

I felt Candy snuggle up to my back, but ignored her as I dropped off to sleep.

***

The sun was warm on my skin where I laid on a chaise on a deserted white sand beach. The water roared gently in the background, offering a cool breeze to counterpoint the heat of the day.

I was in a black bikini, not unlike the one I'd originally made for my caked candy corn hooker, down to the thong, leaving my ass uncovered. It was that detail that told me I had to be dreaming. I was comfortable in my body with my stretch marks and rounded belly and thighs. I had long ago accepted I would be stared at with my stretch marks and cellulite. I did typically wear a bikini, but nothing would make me wear a thong in public.

"I figured it was only fair." I jerked up and turned toward the voice I had come to know so well, but instead of the candy corn body I was used to was someone like I'd never seen before.

She was tall. Taller than my five-nine even. That was clear even while she was stretched out on her own chaise. Her hair was a deep crimson and fell nearly to her waist in hundreds of braids. Silver bands circled a number of them, glinting in the sunlight. She was lean and muscular in a way I rarely appreciated before, but I couldn't help but notice now. Her skin was black as midnight, her eyes bright sapphires that nearly glowed in their intensity.

Those eyes were locked on me and I fought down a blush for having been caught staring at her. I couldn't help it. Not only was she like no human I'd ever seen, she was gorgeous like art.

"What's fair?" I asked, struggling to think straight.

"Putting you in the same clothes you graced me with." A deep purple tongue swept across her lavender lips as her eyes dropped down my body. "Plus, I'm terrible at denying myself things I want."

The implication that she wanted me both made my heart race like a terrified rabbit and sent a jolt of pleasure straight to my clit. She may have been playing normal the last few weeks, but she was a demon and I couldn't let myself forget that.

I kept repeating the thought to myself as Candy got up and moved to kneel beside my chaise. She didn't touch me, but I could feel the heat from her body, burning hotter than the sun. She smelled like cloves and cinnamon, and my entire body leaned toward her until I realized what I'd done and jerked back.

"Oh, little human. I'm not going to hurt you." A large hand cupped my cheek gently. Her thumb stroked slowly across my cheekbone, leaving a trail of fire in its wake. "I'm going to keep you safe for as long as I can have you."

"It's your job." I muttered, barely moving, unsure if it was because I was too terrified of angering the demon or afraid if I did, it would break whatever moment this was.

"My job is to keep you alive and to deliver your soul to Lucifer should you fail to find your true love. Keeping you safe is entirely for my own pleasure and peace of mind." Her thumb touched my lower lip briefly before returning to rest on my cheek.

I sunk my teeth into that lip, afraid to ask the next question but knowing I wouldn't be able to avoid it.

"Why?"

"I can't seem to help myself. You're weak and frail, and yet somehow unerringly kind in a way I have rarely seen before. You care. About everyone and everything. You cry over books and commercials that aren't even sad. It's a little ridiculous, but I can't stop myself from wanting to make you feel better. To keep you safe. To make you mine."

My eyes flew to hers, dark brown to sapphire, and the look there was all heat. This strong demon with centuries of life and terrifying powers was on her knees for me. It was a powerful feeling. My already racing heart sped even faster as I leaned forward and pressed my lips to hers.

That was all the permission Candy needed. Her firm lips moved over mine, pressing them to open for her while her hand moved from my face to my hair. I gasped when she fisted the strands tightly and it was all the invitation she needed. Her tongue swept into my mouth, wet and seeking.

She pushed her torso against my knees and I opened for her, letting her slide her broad body between my legs to press up against me. She wrapped her free arm around my lower back and yanked to pull me to the edge of the chaise so all of me was pressed against all of her. Her arm held me there. I was trapped, couldn't move. Could hardly breathe with the way she was assaulting my mouth. I was already gasping when she finally released my hair, only to slide it down my neck to my chest, where she gently circled my already hard nipple.

"You're so sensitive here." She gently plucked at the bud before pinching it tightly. I cried out, my head falling back. She took advantage and leaned forward to kiss along the column of my neck.

My grip on her arms tightened nearly to the point of painful, but she didn't seem to notice. She continued to kiss her way down my neck to my chest before moving the tiny triangle of fabric out of the way to take my nipple into her hot mouth.

The heat was intense and unlike anything I'd ever felt before. I jerked away, but immediately grabbed her head to hold her to me when she tried to pull away. The different sensations of wet and hot and hard, was driving me insane. When I loosened my grip a little she moved to my other breast, lavishing it with attention.

When I was a writhing mess, she helped lower me back, so I was lying on the chaise properly. I pulled her down to me to kiss, and she came with a smile. Her body was warm and solid as she climbed on top of me.

I gasped as she pulled away from me. "No!"

"Shh now, little human. I'll take good care of you." Her voice was gravel, low and rough and tugged at me.

She slid down the chaise until she was kneeling between my splayed legs. I knew I had to look a mess with my hair in snarls from her hands, my boobs flopping around with the useless triangle bikini top yanked to the sides and my chest heaving trying to get a solid breath. Candy didn't seem to mind. She looked at me like I was the biggest piece of double fudge chocolate cake and she was going to eat me whole.

I arched into her hand as she trailed two fingers down my slit from the outside of my bottoms. Her hands moved to trail up my thighs to the ties on either side of my hips and in seconds, she had the knots undone and my bottoms off.

"So fucking wet for me already." This time when she slid her fingers over me, they came away wet.

She sucked them into her mouth and moaned. "So sweet. I'm going to eat you whole."

For a second, I wondered if she meant that literally; she was a demon after all. But then her head ducked down and her thick tongue was sliding the same path as her fingers, licking me like an ice cream cone. The movement was too soft and too shallow to give me the pressure I needed, and I tilted my hips up in frustration. Silently begging her for more.

"Ah, ah, ah, little human. Use your words." Her grin was feral as she slid her body down to lay her upper torso on the chaise so her face was even with my cunt. "Tell me what you need."

"Lick me." I pleaded, arching toward her.

She did. Once. One long and gentle lick along my seam, not giving me any more than the last taste had. I groaned, so frustrated and hot, and my pussy was begging to be touched.

My pussy may be needy, but I wasn't going to beg. I shifted and reached one hand down to touch myself but before I could both hands were restrained and pulled up above my head, leaving me stretched out.

"No touching. This pretty cunt is all mine. Now tell me what you want, little human. Tell me and I'll give you everything you need."

"Make me come. Lick my cunt, suck my clit, fuck me until I'm screaming." I begged, writhing in the invisible bonds and under the weight of Candy's hands on my thighs.

"Good girl," Candy murmured, before lowering her head again.

This time, her tongue speared through my outer lips to the damp, sensitive skin below. She started circling my opening before moving up to press firmly against my clit. She stayed there for a long moment, licking and sucking, and generally driving me out of my mind before shifting down to spear her tongue into me.

My fingers pressed hard into the top of the chaise as she devoured me. The intense heat of her mouth adding to the sensations in a way no human could ever compare to. I was dancing on the knife's edge of orgasm when she suddenly sucked my clit into her hot mouth, at the same time she speared a long finger inside of me.

My body arched, my inner muscles clenched tight, my moan could only be described as pornographic.

Chapter Eight

I slammed into consciousness, my body damp and aching and on the edge of orgasm. I could feel the phantom sensations of Candy's hands and mouth on me.

Desperate for release, I shoved my hand into my panties, seeking out that swollen bundle of nerves that was physically aching for attention. I rubbed firm and fast but I couldn't get over that edge. Couldn't find the release I was so desperate for.

"Use me," Candy's voice said from the end of the bed. "Please, I'm begging you, use me."

I didn't allow myself time to think. I just reached down and grabbed her, stuffing the stuffed candy corn between my legs as I rolled over to my stomach. I shifted until my clit made contact. I groaned as pleasure coursed through me.

I came up to my knees, keeping up the nearly frantic grind as I moved. In seconds, I had my dress over my head and my hands on my breasts, kneading the sensitive flesh.

"Yes, touch yourself for me. Ride me. Get off on me." Candy's voice was grit and gravel, low and deeper than I'd ever heard it and it wound me higher knowing she was getting pleasure from this too.

I slammed both hands to the headboard. The change in position sent a zing of pleasure through me, and I used the position to help grind down harder.

From there, it only took seconds before pleasure exploded over me. I whined as my pussy clenched on nothing as my orgasm flowed over me, but I didn't want to stop grinding my oh so very sensitive clit against Candy's firm body.

It took minutes for me to come down from the high of my orgasm. It took seconds for the embarrassment to kick in.

I scrambled off of Candy and my bed, grabbing for the towel I'd left on the floor after getting dressed for my date earlier. I wasn't sure my limbs were stable enough to work through getting me back into my dress. That was the hardest I've ever come, and I'd done it while grinding on a demon-possessed stuffed toy.

What the hell had I been thinking?

"What did you do to me?" I asked, my voice rough and low, forced past the tightening in my throat.

"Nothing you didn't beg for." Candy sounded tense as she worked her way to her feet. Something that normally made me smile in its awkwardness, but only set a stone in my stomach this time. "Nothing we didn't both want."

"You caused that. You fed off of me!" My limbs were still shaking as I stood there and struggled to make sense of what had just happened. I was twenty-seven years old, I didn't grind on stuffed animals like a pubescent first learning about pleasure.

"I didn't take more than you gave me." Candy defended. "I didn't do anything you didn't want. So you're okay with my true demon form, but not this monstrosity you created for me?"

I couldn't answer that because in a big way, it was true. The Candy in my dreams had been a gorgeous and glorious being. The Candy I knew was more than a little ridiculous. But I wasn't prepared to deal with that, so I turned.

"How? How were you in my dream? How did you…" I could not even bring myself to finish the sentence. The idea was so insane.

But I knew without a shadow of a doubt, that it had been Candy in my dream. Candy in her true form. That magnificent gorgeous creature had been reduced to the ridiculous because of me. "There are so many things I can do that you can't even imagine. Coming to someone in their dreams is child's play for a demon like me. But here's the thing, Clover. I can't make someone give in to me. Everything we did, was because you wanted it."

"You're a demon. You're probably lying." Except a part of me didn't think she was. Other than her true purpose here, I didn't think she'd lied to me about anything since she arrived. She'd been nothing but blunt and painfully honest about everything, from her thoughts in my taste of entertainment to my clothing.

While I knew there was more to her presence here than being my fairy godmother in my mission to find true love, I didn't think she'd lied about much else. And deep down, I knew she wasn't lying about this. I had wanted her when she was in her true demon form. It hadn't felt coerced or forced. It hadn't been because of some magic.

Candy and I had formed a very strange relationship over the last month, one that was nearly friendship. If you could be friends with the demon tasked with stealing your soul.

Except, she never did anything against me. She'd done nothing but encourage me to go out and meet people. She'd helped me pick clothing and tried to make me look my best.

"Little human, I have never once lied to you. Not once since I've been here." Candy's voice was low and firm. When I looked back at her, she was gone.

Chapter Nine

Candy managed to avoid me the rest of the weekend. By Monday, I was starting to miss her. She was snarky and sarcastic and funny, and I'd enjoyed her company more than I could have imagined.

Since my parents moved south to warmer weather and my grandma died, leaving me her house, it had been just me. I'd liked having someone else around to talk with while I worked on making new patterns and fulfilling orders. I missed her constant narration of the shows I watched and her unironic love of baking shows.

Monday afternoon I managed to hunt her down in my spare bedroom where I ran my business out of. She was lying on a pile of stuffies waiting to be mailed out.

"I'm sorry." I told the demon. She didn't move, but I knew she was hearing me. "I was a jerk, and you didn't deserve it."

I dropped down on the floor and laid my head next to hers in the pile of stuffies. I poked her side, but she still didn't respond.

"You were right. You didn't do anything to me that I didn't ask for, and I wouldn't ask for again, if given the chance. You were also right that it was bullshit for me to be okay with your demon form and not the poppet I put you into. That was cruel and small of me. Forgive me?"

I blinked puppy dog eyes at her and she broke, laughing at me.

"I forgive you." She said, haughtily before shifting closer and snuggling into me. "I can't exactly blame you for not liking this comedic form. Honestly, Clover? What were you thinking?"

"That it would be funny. And it was, until it was possessed by a succubus." I turned onto my side and draped an arm over Candy, pulling her closer to me. "I don't know if you've somehow managed to miss this, but I make my career on being more than a little ridiculous with yarn."

"Oh, little human, we're laying on a pile of multi-color penises. It was really hard to miss." I burst out laughing, feeling better than I had in days.

***

We fell back into an easy habit after that, with one exception. Every night Candy came to me in my dreams in her glorious demon form and gave me more pleasure than my body knew what to do with.

A few days into our new relationship a large package arrived holding a variety of sex toys from tiny bullet vibrators to scarily large dildos, I was confident no one could actually use.

"Don't worry, we'll start small." Candy assured me, nudging through the box with her feet.

She helped me break through my shyness by starting. When she could touch me and wind me up, before waking me up with my skin hot and tight and my body wet and aching for release. I couldn't care about being shy when I was so desperate to be touched. She would somehow already have a toy at hand for me to grab for release.

I'd come hard, exhausted and sated. Candy would feed on my release and become energized. I started waking up in the morning to breakfast ready for me, though she never got any better at making coffee. I started using the single-cup maker I'd bought when it became a fad before I realized I drank more coffee than made sense.

We would watch TV and movies, emphasis on baking shows. Candy had become addicted to them since coming topside and I just liked having noise on in the background as I worked.

I eventually got around to posting photos of Candy in her natural hooker state, and she immediately became a wildly popular pattern. Not only did I sell the pattern for others to make, but I had endless requests to make them for people who didn't have the skill or time. Everyone thought her popularity was hysterical.

The one issue with my new normal was the fact that I had only eleven months to find my true love or Satan would claim my soul. I was having such a good time with Candy I had no interest in going out and finding someone else. I'd spend nights out at the bar with my friends thinking about her, and how long until I could get home to her. I avoided going out whenever possible.

Why would I want someone else when she made me comfortable and brought me more pleasure than anyone in my entire history had?

Chapter Ten

"I know you said I needed to keep dating," I called out to Candy as I walked into the house from yet another terrible first date. "But I don't know that I can keep doing this."

I dropped my keys into the bowl on the entry table and flipped the lock before toeing off my flats and heading into the living room where I expected to find Candy watching the latest season of her favorite baking show. The TV was on but there was no sign of my favorite candy corn. I wandered the house trying to figure out where she was hiding, assuming she was playing some sort of game.

I eventually found her in my room on the bed.

"Waiting for me? What if it would have been true love and I would have brought her home with me?" There had been zero chance of that. The date had been a bust, and not a small part of that was due to the demon on my bed.

Candy didn't say anything. I sighed and flopped down on the bed next to her. "Look, I know it sucks, but we both agreed that I have to keep trying to find my true love or I'm going to end up in hell and neither of us want that. You know I'd much rather be here with you."

I nudged her, and she went flying off the bed, as if she was nothing but yarn and fluff. I scrambled off the bed and grabbed her, but the stuffy was missing the normal weight she'd always had. She may make herself lighter or heavier based on what she wanted, but she'd never once felt as light and inconsequential as the stuffy should have felt.

"Candy?" I shook the doll, but there was no response. "Candy, this isn't funny."

Still nothing. I shook her and yelled at her, begged her to talk to me, but eventually, I had to accept what I knew from the moment she fell off the bed. The demon no longer inhabited the stuffed candy corn. She was gone.

"No, no, no, no, no, no." I cried, dropping the candy corn on the bed and digging my phone from my pants pocket. I hit Violet on speed dial.

"How was your date?" She asked, her voice light.

"Violet, I need your help. Candy is gone." I was nearly hysterical, squeezing the stuffy close to my chest. "I got home from my date and the stuffy was just empty and Candy is gone, and I don't know how to get her back."

"Isn't that a good thing? Clove? Doesn't that mean you found your true love?"

She wasn't getting it.

"Candy was my true love!" I screamed into the phone.

There was a beat of silence as we both took in what I said. I hadn't thought about it, but the moment the words came out I knew they were true. Candy was the one being I loved on this planet and now she was gone, and I would never be okay again.

"I'll be right there."

"Bring your book. We're summoning the devil."

***

"Are you sure you want to do this?" Violet asked as she set up a summoning circle. "I'm not even sure this is going to work, and it might make things worse. Plus, you're asking me to summon the actual devil. This has never ended well for anyone in the history of cinema."

"I don't give a shit. I need her back." I was sitting on the floor watching Violet, unable to move. "I never told her."

"Never told her what, honey?" Violet asked, setting the salt back on my counter and grabbing a lighter and a bunch of candles.

"That I loved her. I never told her I loved her and now she's gone and she'll never know."

"You know how crazy that sounds, Clove?"

"I don't care! I don't care how crazy I sound. You don't understand. You can't possibly understand. She was different, okay?"

Violet nodded but didn't say anything as she set the five black pillar candles around the circle and lit each one. She handed me a knife and a small glass measuring bowl. I sliced against my palm and held it over the bowl until the blood slowed. We exchanged a kitchen towel for the bowl and Violet moved to the circle while I pressed the towel against my hand.

Violet dipped her fingers into the bowl and flung my blood at the circle. At first it looked like nothing was happening, but as Violet chanted the incantation, the salt circle began to glow a light blue color. The air inside the circle began to shimmer like hot air over a parking lot on a hot day.

Slowly, a man shimmered into existence. He started as the hazy outline of a ghost and slowly solidified to a towering black man with coal-black eyes wearing a well-tailored black suit. A black shirt and black tie completed the black on black on black look. It would have been sexy as hell had a) the air not been simmering with barely restrained violence and b) I didn't know I was staring at the actual devil.

"You dare summon me?" His glare was on Violet, who was visibly shaking in her shoes where she stood just outside the circle. Giant bully.

"You're goddamn right I dare," I said, launching to my feet to stand in front of Violet. "You took Candy. Give her back."

He eyed me up and down in a way that made my skin crawl. It wasn't a sexual perusal, but felt like he was debating the best, most effective way to peel my skin from my bones. Still, I refused to back down.

"Callaxis is back where she belongs. Her job has been completed. She failed to procure your soul." Lucifer started to fade.

"No!" I stepped forward, but Violet pulled me back to keep me from breaking the salt circle. She kept one arm around my stomach, grounding me to her and to my spot on the floor. "She may not have claimed my soul, but she has my heart. Our bargain was to find my true love, right? Well, I found her and it's Candy. You have to give her back or you've reneged on your bargain."

"Careful, Clover," Violet whispered behind me.

"Fuck careful." I wiped my eyes with the back of my hand. "Give her back."

"I don't take demands from mere humans." Lucifer said, his voice haughty. "Do not call me again."

The pressure in the room swelled until my ears popped.

He was gone.

I dropped to the floor, taking Violet with me. Tears streamed from my eyes as I stared blankly at the center of the summoning circle.

I had lost Candy.

Chapter Eleven

Violet saw me to the couch and wrapped a blanket around me before cleaning up the summoning supplies. She was reluctant to leave, but I turned on Candy's favorite baking show and told her I would be fine.

I was lying.

She knew it.

I would never be fine again.

"I can't believe you're watching this without me." A low, smoky voice said from behind me. I struggled to my feet, the blanket tangling around my legs, causing me to trip and land on the coffee table.

There, leaning against the doorway to the living room, in all of her demony glory, was Candy. Her black body clad in a deep crimson dress with a slit up to her hip. The strapless sweetheart neckline was defying gravity. Her braids together in a long plait over one shoulder.

I sat on the table staring at her, completely unable to move. To process the fact she was here, really here.

"Are you going to say something or just sit there staring at me?"

"How?" I got out through my tight throat.

She pushed off the wall and stalked toward me. "You made a deal with the devil, and Lucifer always keeps his word."

I snort-laughed before bursting into sobs. I couldn't believe she was here with me. I couldn't believe she was here as herself. I hadn't believed I would ever have this.

In a flash, she was next to me, kneeling beside the table and taking my face in her hands. "No, don't cry."

I launched myself at her. Gripping her broad shoulders in my hands, I smashed my lips to hers. She hesitated for the barest of seconds before kissing me back at full force. Her hand moved to my hair, tugging my head back for a better angle to deepen the kiss. Her other hand skimmed up the outside of my thigh and under my skirt.

Where she had been heat in my dreams she was now fire. Where she had been soft and smooth her palm was now rough. The skin beneath my hands was leathery, rather than soft like human skin. These small differences meant everything. They meant I was not dreaming.

"More," I panted, pushing the top of her dress down to find her breasts. They were large with large nipples, but seemed to lack any areola. I didn't mind. Every part of Candy was perfect to me.

Candy released my hair and moved both hands to the button at the front of my dress. She worked her fingers under the edges of the material before ripping it clear in half. I moaned, ridiculously turned on by the display of brute strength. Candy dipped her head, taking my nipple into her hot mouth and it was my turn to dig fingers into hair as I kept her in place.

She tolerated it for only a moment before she drew my hands out and behind my back. They were restrained there, without the use of any ties or restraints. I raised my eyebrows at Candy.

"I don't just have power in your dreams." Her grin was feral as she lowered me back onto the coffee table, licking her way down my body.

"But I want to touch you," I whined, wiggling to get comfortable and also see if the invisible binds would come loose.

"Soon, my love." Candy held up a hand to show claws that had never been there in the past, before using them to shred my underwear off my body. "I need the taste of you on my tongue. I've been craving it since our first night together. Dream you was delicious. I'm certain real you will be close to the divine."

My only response was a moan. She didn't play or hesitate this time, diving her tongue into my slit, licking fire along my pussy. Her mouth was hotter than it had been in the dreams, her tongue forked at the tip, allowing her to slide it around my clit and flutter her tongue, sending me over the edge.

I was just coming down when she speared me with her tongue, forcing the thick length of it into my clenching cunt. Her thumb found my sensitive clit and rubbed slow circles as she fucked me with her tongue. Her mouth was heat and fire and the sensations together overwhelmed me.

"Let go, my love," Candy said, pulling back. Her warm breath was fire on my damp flesh, her thumb increased in pressure and speed. "Come for me."

My entire body grew tight, liquid pleasure pooled low in my stomach. My body arched and ached. I fought my bonds, desperate to touch her. Still, she pressed on, rubbing and circling that little pleasure button until I couldn't take it anymore.

I shattered, screaming her name.

My Candy.

My one true love.

My everything.

Epilogue

"They're staring at you again," I complained, spinning my margarita glass back and forth between my hands. The men at the next table over hadn't been able to keep their eyes off of her all night.

"I can't help it." Candy whispered in my ear. "Lust demon."

I harrumphed.

"You're cute when you're jealous." She nipped my earlobe.

I glared at her before taking a large drink of margarita. We were out with the girls, still trying to find their true loves before it was too late. Candy was in her human form, which was a tall, willowy white woman with blond hair, cornflower blue eyes, and an hourglass figure men would kill to get at and women would kill to have. I supposed that was the point, to be an object of lust so she could feed on them. But I was learning that I had a jealousy streak a mile wide and didn't like this version of Candy. I missed her true demon form whenever we went out.

"Will you guys stop?" Jasmine asked, snagging a fried pickle from the tray in front of us. "I cannot handle the level of sweet happening over there. It's going to make me puke."

"I would hate to have you regurgitate on the table." Candy said, leaning away from me and sitting upright in her chair.

"Let her." I said, moving to sit on Candy's lap and tossing an arm around her shoulders. "She's just upset because her demon finally showed up and nearly got caught by the kids."

Knowing that it would, Jasmine went off in a rant about stupid men, demons and humans, and how they were all just useless. Pointing out that at least Candy cooked for me and took care of the house so I could focus on making orders and writing up my patterns.

It was true, Candy was pretty much perfect. She'd offered to get a job, but I honestly liked having her around all day. She took over the day to day part of my business: shipping orders, customer emails, and the like. Giving me more time to do what I do best. We were a team. And I wouldn't have wanted it any other way.

"I love you, too," she whispered in my ear.

"I told you to stop reading my mind." I pressed a soft kiss to her mouth. "I love you more."

Sure, Candy wasn't who I envisioned all those weeks ago when we'd cast the spell, but she was exactly who I needed to complete me.

Author's Note

Thank you so much for taking a chance on a new author and my off-the-wall little story. I really hope you enjoyed Corny and will consider coming back for the rest of the gang as they meet their demons and find their true love. If not, I don't blame you, this was a little out there even for me. But it was a lot of fun to write and if you made it this far, well, frankly, I'm impressed.

To J, A, E, B & C - I literally couldn't have done this without your support and encouragement. Thanks for listening to me say "I'm going to write smut about a caked-out candy corn" and going "Hell Yeah you are!" instead of calling the people with the butterfly nets, as you probably should have done.

To Mom - I'm sorry. I hope you never read this and learn just how deranged your child actually is. But if you do, remember you raised me and have no one to blame but yourself.

And to you, dear reader, for making it this far. You're the light of my life, the wind beneath my wings, the air I breathe. I don't know, I'm out of sappy references but know that I freaking love you.

Printed in Great Britain
by Amazon

30550282R00040